All aboard the Story Train!

Hello! Let's see who's
in Story Corner today.

Hello Lily
and Milly!

Hello Hip and Hop!

Hello Loopy!

It's time for a story and I know just the book.

Are you sitting down comfy
and ready to listen?

This story is called "The Stripy Seed".
It is written by Gillian Corderoy and
the pictures are by Rebecca Elgar.

The
Stripy Seed

Written by Gillian Corderoy

Illustrated by Rebecca Elgar

Let's begin.

One day Karima found a little stripy seed.

She planted it carefully in a pot, then watched it and waited for it to grow.

Karima watered it . . . and waited . . .

I can't wait to see what Karima grows!

and waited . . .

One day a tiny green
shoot appeared.
Karima watered
it and talked to it.

Seeds need water
to help them
grow.

The tiny green shoot grew two little leaves.
"Soon it will make a flower," she thought.

The plant kept on growing taller
and taller and taller.

"There must be something at the top,"
thought Karima.

She started to climb
up and up and up
through the clouds.

That looks
fun! I like
climbing too.

When she got right
to the very top . . .

Karima played until all the stars came out.
Then she slid back down through the
leaves and home to bed.

Sliding is
fun!

Karima played with her sunflower all summer.

But one day when she ran outside,
the leaves had fallen from the stalk.
Karima couldn't climb up.

Karima really missed her sunflower friend.
She sat day after day, looking at the pot.

Pitter-patter,
pitter-patter.

Then one day, little stripy raindrops fell
all around her, settling on the ground.

Karima picked one up. It wasn't a little stripy raindrop, it was a little stripy seed!

Karima has lots of stripy seeds!

She collected all the
seeds and planted
them carefully
into pots.

She watered them and watched them.

And before too long,
Karima was playing
with lots of flowery
friends again.

Did you enjoy the story?

It's time to show me the story!

Pretend to plant a seed just like Karima.

Now climb up your giant plant. Move your arms and legs as you get higher and higher!

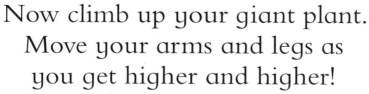

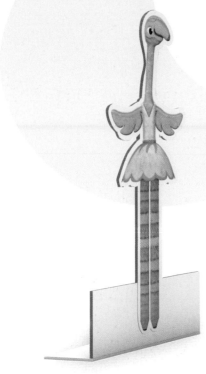

Can you stretch up
like a tall sunflower?

Wheee!

What would it be like to
bounce on a sunflower?
Jump up and down just
like Karima did!

It's time to go, but come back soon
because we all love stories!

All aboard the Story Train!

First published 2010 by Campbell Books
an imprint of Macmillan Children's Books
a division of Macmillan Publishers Ltd
20 New Wharf Road, London N1 9RR
Basingstoke and Oxford
www.panmacmillan.com
Associated companies worldwide
ISBN 978-0-330-52511-4
© Story Train Distribution FZ-LLC 2010
A 3Line Media production in association with
twofour54 for CBeebies
Design and setting © 2010 Macmillan Publishers Ltd
Printed in Italy
1 2 3 4 5 6 7 8 9